ASTRID
& APOLLO

AND THE
SOCCER CELEBRATION

BY
V.T. BIDANIA

ILLUSTRATED BY
DARA LASHIA LEE

PICTURE WINDOW BOOKS
a capstone imprint

For Kai and Siri — V.T.B.

Astrid and Apollo is published by Picture Window Books,
an imprint of Capstone.
1710 Roe Crest Drive
North Mankato, Minnesota 56003
www.capstonepub.com

Library of Congress Cataloging-in-Publication Data

Names: Bidania, V. T., author. | Lee, Dara Lashia, illustrator.
Title: Astrid and Apollo and the soccer celebration / by V.T. Bidania ;
    illustrated by Dara Lashia Lee.
Description: North Mankato, Minnesota : Picture Window Books, a Capstone
    imprint, [2020] | Series: Astrid and Apollo | Audience: Ages 6-8. |
    Summary: Twins Astrid and Apollo are excited to be going to the Hmong
    July Fourth Soccer Festival, but when they are told to babysit their
    baby sister, Eliana, it looks like they will miss the particular match
    their father is interested in—especially as they cannot figure out what
    the "yummy milk" Eliana demands is, and are forced to spend their money
    on buying different treats to keep her from throwing a tantrum.
Identifiers: LCCN 2019057134 (print) | LCCN 2019057135 (ebook) |
    ISBN 9781515861249 (hardcover) | ISBN 9781515861331 (paperback) |
    ISBN 9781515861348 (adobe pdf)
Subjects: LCSH: Hmong American children—Juvenile fiction. | Hmong American
    families—Juvenile fiction. | Twins—Juvenile fiction. | Brothers and
    sisters—Juvenile fiction. | Fourth of July—Juvenile fiction. | Ethnic
    festivals—Juvenile fiction. | CYAC: Hmong Americans—Fiction. |
    Twins—Fiction. | Brothers and sisters—Fiction. | Festivals—Fiction. |
    Soccer—Fiction.
Classification: LCC PZ7.1.B5333 As 2020 (print) | LCC PZ7.1.B5333 (ebook)
    | DDC [Fic]—dc23
LC record available at https://lccn.loc.gov/2019057134
LC ebook record available at https://lccn.loc.gov/2019057135

Design Elements: Shutterstock: Ingo Menhard, Yangxiong

Designer: Lori Bye

Table of Contents

Hi, I'm Astrid. My twin brother is Apollo, and we were born in Minnesota. We live here with our mom, dad, and little sister, Eliana.

ASTRID GAO NOU

Hi, I'm Apollo! Our mom and dad were both born in Laos. They came to the United States when they were very young and grew up here.

APOLLO NOU KOU

MOM, DAD, AND ELIANA GAO CHEE

HMONG WORDS

gao (GOW)—girl; it is often placed in front of a girl's name. Hmong spelling: *nkauj*

Gao Chee (GOW chee)—shiny girl. Hmong spelling: *Nkauj Ci*

Gao Nou (GOW new)—sun girl. Hmong spelling: *Nkauj Hnub*

Hmong (MONG)—a group of people who came to the U.S. from Laos. Many Hmong from Laos now live in Minnesota. Hmong spelling: *Hmoob*

Nou Kou (NEW koo)—star. Hmong spelling: *Hnub Qub*

tou (TOO)—boy or son; it is often placed in front of a boy's name. Hmong spelling: *tub*

CHAPTER 1

Cucumber Shake

"On your mark," said Astrid.

"Get set," said Apollo.

"Go!" said Astrid. She ran as fast as she could.

Apollo ran next to her. They were running from one side of the yard to the other.

All of a sudden, Eliana came out of the house. She hurried in their direction.

"Watch out!" said Astrid. She quickly stepped to the side.

Apollo moved too. "Careful!" he said. But Eliana kept running.

Astrid and Apollo slowed down and stopped.

Eliana stood right in front of them. "Go!" she said, smiling.

Astrid took a big breath. She put her hands on her knees. "You're silly, Eliana! I almost won!" she said.

"Why did you do that?" Apollo asked Eliana. She laughed.

"And I was ahead of you, Astrid!" he added.

"You were not!" said Astrid.

"Eliana, there you are," said Mom. She walked over from the car.

"Are we going to the festival now?" asked Astrid.

"Yes, it's time to go," Mom said. She carried Eliana to the car and helped her into the car seat. Mom got in and stuck her head out the car window. "Astrid and Apollo, are you coming?" she asked.

Astrid looked at Apollo. "Race you?"

Apollo nodded.

Astrid ran quickly. Apollo was close behind. Astrid got to the car and pulled open the door.

Apollo hurried to the other side. He opened his door. He sat down just as Astrid sat on her seat.

"I win!" said Astrid.

"It's a tie!" Apollo said.

Mom turned around from the front seat. "Ready, everyone?" she said.

Astrid and Apollo laughed. "Yes!" they said.

It was the first day of the July Fourth Soccer Festival. Astrid and Apollo were excited. They wanted to watch the soccer games. They wanted to eat at the food booths. And they really wanted to run around the huge park.

Suddenly, Eliana said, "Yummy!"

Astrid turned to her. "What's yummy?" she asked.

"Milk," said Eliana.

"I forgot Eliana's snack bag in the house," said Mom. She got out of the car and handed Apollo a small bowl and spoon. "Please give her cucumbers. She can have her milk later."

"I'll feed her," said Astrid.

Apollo gave the bowl to Astrid. She took off the lid. "Have some cucumber shake," she said.

Apollo smiled and pointed a thumb at his chest. "I called it that first. Now everyone's saying it," he said.

"Because that's what it is!" said Astrid.

Apollo came up with the name cucumber shake. Mom made it by cutting a cucumber in half. She took out the seeds. Then she scraped out the insides with a spoon. She mixed the insides in a bowl with sugar. Dad said this was a Hmong dish for grandmothers, but Eliana loved it anyway.

Astrid fed a spoon of the cucumber to Eliana.

Eliana shook her head and said, "Milk."

"Cucumber," said Astrid.

"Milk!" Eliana said. She hit the tray
on her car seat.

Apollo held onto her hands. "You
can have milk later," he said.

Eliana ignored him and said,
"Yummy!"

Mom came back into the car and sat down. "It seems Eliana doesn't want cucumbers. Please put it away, Astrid. Let's go," she said.

Mom turned on the car. Astrid put the lid on the bowl. Eliana started to cry.

"Please be nice," said Apollo. "The soccer festival is going to be so fun. Okay?"

Eliana stopped crying. She screamed, "YUMMY MILK!"

Astrid and Apollo covered their ears.

"Eliana, stop that *right now*," Mom said.

Eliana stopped.

Astrid and Apollo shook their heads.

"By the way, I need you to take care of Eliana at the festival," Mom said.

Apollo opened his mouth in surprise. "What?" he said.

"Can't she stay with you, Mom?" Astrid asked.

"We told Dad we'd watch soccer with him," said Apollo. "His favorite team is playing."

Dad was already at the park. He went early to watch the first games. Dad wanted to see his team win and celebrate. Astrid and Apollo wanted to celebrate with him.

"I'm helping Auntie May at her papaya salad booth," Mom said. "I won't have time to watch Eliana."

One of the best parts about the festival was the food booths. They sold tasty snacks, desserts, and drinks. Everyone loved eating papaya salad. That meant Auntie May's booth would be very busy.

Apollo moved up in his seat. "But we want to have a celebration with Dad," he said. "He says the Twisty Typhoons will win the final game."

"Wait," said Astrid. "Wasn't the team called the Wild Whirlpools?"

"Mom, what's the name of Dad's favorite team?" Apollo said.

"It's the Howling Hurricanes," said Mom. "And you can take Eliana with you to watch them."

Astrid and Apollo frowned. They wouldn't be able to run around the park if they had Eliana with them.

"Maybe she'll take a nap," said Apollo.

"We can't go fast with her stroller," Astrid said.

Apollo shrugged. "We can just watch soccer, then. We'll race another time."

CHAPTER 2

Sweet Snowflakes

When they got to the park, Astrid and Apollo followed Mom and Eliana to the food booths. The booths were lined up at the top of a hill. It was very sunny.

"It's too hot. Let's go under that big tree for shade. We can look for Auntie May later," said Mom.

As they stood under the tree, Astrid saw Auntie May. She was at her booth nearby. "She's right there!" said Astrid.

They left the tree and walked up to her booth.

"Hello!" said Auntie May. "Kids, your dad left this note for you. His phone battery ran out. He said to look for him at this field."

"Thank you," said Mom. She took off her sunglasses to read Dad's note. She turned the note around. "It says number six. Do you see field six?"

Astrid and Apollo looked down at the soccer fields. Each field had a big white sign with a black number.

Apollo saw field six. It was the middle field next to a tall pole. "I see it!" he said. "It's by that pole. Look at all those people!"

Crowds of people sat on the grass watching the games. The people held colorful umbrellas. The umbrellas gave them shade from the hot sun.

Astrid liked all the different colors of the umbrellas. They looked pretty on the bright green grass. "The umbrellas look like rainbow dots," she said.

Apollo nodded. "Rainbow dots everywhere!"

All over the park, hundreds of people walked around. They were talking with family and friends. They were eating and taking pictures and videos.

"I can't wait to see the soccer players do headers. Like this," Apollo said. He jumped and quickly moved his head up.

"I want to see them do bicycle kicks!" Astrid said.

"Like this?" said Apollo. He jumped again and kicked his leg to the side. He fell and rolled on the grass.

Astrid laughed. "Like that, but better!" she said.

"Now kids, if you need me, come back to Auntie May's booth," said Mom. "Look for the big tree or the sign."

A huge pink sign was above the booth. It said *Auntie May's Papaya Salad.*

"Yes, Mom," said Astrid.

"Look for the tall pole to find Dad," said Mom.

Apollo nodded. "Okay, Mom."

"Yummy milk," Eliana said in a sad voice.

Mom gave them some money. "This is for snacks. There's a lot of food here, so try what you like. But the lines can be long. After you eat, go find your dad," she said.

"Kids, take some papaya salad!" said Auntie May. She was wearing an apron that was pink like the sign. She gave them a bowl with two forks.

Apollo could smell the lime from the salad. "Smells good," he said.

Astrid saw pieces of red pepper in the bowl. "How many peppers are in here?" she asked.

"Don't worry, it's not spicy," said Auntie May. She held up three fingers. "Only three peppers."

"Thanks, Auntie May," said Astrid. She put the bowl in the stroller's cup holder.

"Bye, kids," said Mom. "Take good care of your baby sister!"

"Bye, Mom. We will," they said and left Auntie May's booth.

Astrid opened a yellow umbrella. She held it above them. Apollo pushed Eliana's stroller.

They walked down the row of food booths.

It was crowded and hot. Most of the booths had long lines of people waiting.

Astrid set the umbrella down and gave Apollo one of the forks. He stopped the stroller. They both tried a bite of the salad.

Astrid's face turned red. "It's really spicy!" she said.

Apollo blew air out of his mouth. "Why did Auntie May say it's *not* spicy? My mouth is on fire!"

"It's not spicy to her!" said Astrid. She fanned her mouth with her hand.

"I need something cold to drink!" said Apollo.

Eliana looked at the salad. "Yummy," she said.

"No, this is too spicy for you," said Astrid. She put the salad under the stroller seat.

Up ahead, Astrid saw a booth selling shaved ice. "Sweet snowflakes!" she said. That was the name Astrid had made up for shaved ice.

Beside it was a booth selling ice pops. Next to that was a booth selling ice cream. Both booths had long lines.

"There's no line for shaved ice. Let's get that!" Apollo ran to the booth.

Astrid closed the umbrella and hung it on the side of the stroller. She pushed the stroller and followed Apollo.

Apollo took out some money. He asked for one cup of shaved ice.

The man in the booth put a cup under a machine. He pressed a button and thin ice fell into the cup. It looked like snowflakes. He poured red, green, and yellow syrup over the ice. Then he gave the cup to Apollo.

Apollo handed it to Astrid. She stuck a spoon in the ice and took a bite. She closed her eyes and said, "Sweet snowflakes to the rescue!"

Astrid gave the cup back to Apollo. He took a big bite. "Fire is out!" he said.

"Milk?" Eliana asked.

"This isn't milk," said Apollo.

"Let's give her some anyway," said Astrid.

Apollo fed the ice to Eliana.

Eliana didn't close her mouth. The ice dripped down her chin.

"Don't waste it," Apollo said.

"Yummy," Eliana said again.

"Why does she spit it out but say 'yummy'?" said Apollo.

Astrid wiped Eliana's chin. "Let's just give her milk." She took Eliana's cup of milk from her bag and gave it to her.

Eliana threw the cup to the ground. "Milk!" she cried.

"Stop that. It *is* milk," said Apollo.

Astrid picked up the cup and put it away.

Eliana sat back in her seat. She crossed her arms over her chest.

Astrid and Apollo kept walking. They shared the shaved ice until it was gone.

"I feel hungry now. I want a meal," said Apollo.

"Me too," said Astrid.

"Look! Pho!" said Apollo.

CHAPTER 3

Noodle Bowls

Apollo ran up to the pho noodle booth in front of them. Behind it was a tent filled with long tables. People sat at the tables eating big bowls of noodles in beef soup.

Astrid waited with Eliana while Apollo got in line.

When it was Apollo's turn, he said, "Can I please have one bowl of pho to go?"

The lady at the booth put noodles in a bowl. She poured hot soup over the noodles. She tossed green onions and basil on top.

Apollo handed her some money and said, "Thank you."

When Apollo got back, Astrid looked at the bowl. "Looks great," she said.

Apollo took a sip of the soup. "It tastes great! But hot!"

Astrid pointed to the booth next to them. People were eating bowls of noodles in chicken curry. "Look at the khao poon noodles!" she said.

"You want to buy it?" said Apollo. "I'll wait here with Eliana."

Astrid walked up to the khao poon booth and stood in line. Soon it was her turn. "One bowl of khao poon, please," she said.

The girl at the booth got out a bowl. She poured red curry over the noodles. Astrid smiled at the pieces of chicken in the curry.

"Thanks," Astrid said. She handed her the money. Astrid took the bowl back to the stroller.

Astrid stood beside Apollo. She ate the khao poon. Apollo ate the pho.

"What does it taste like?" Apollo asked.

"Yummy!" said Astrid.

Eliana looked up at them. "Yummy," she said.

"Do you want noodles?" Astrid asked her.

Eliana shook her head.

People walked by holding umbrellas, food, and drinks.

The air was hot and heavy with the smell of food. Astrid and Apollo used napkins to wipe the sweat off their faces.

"We should hurry," said Apollo. He ate a bite of pho. "So we don't miss the game."

Astrid swallowed a bite of khao poon.

"But what about Eliana?" she asked. "We still don't know what she wants to eat."

"Something yummy. Something with milk," said Apollo.

"Wait, we didn't get any barbecued meat!" said Astrid.

A group of kids walked past them. They were carrying barbecued meat on sticks. Astrid and Apollo saw smoke from the grills up ahead. It smelled like a picnic on a sunny day.

"I'll get it," said Astrid. She put her bowl in the cup holder. She hurried to the barbecue booth.

Apollo set his bowl in the cup holder too. He covered both bowls with lids and pushed the stroller behind Astrid.

Astrid bought sticks of grilled beef and pork. She handed them to Apollo.

"Yummy milk," Eliana said.

"Try some," said Apollo.

He took a piece of beef and fed it to Eliana.

Eliana threw it on the grass.

"What if we got her sticky rice?" said Astrid.

"Good idea. I see some there," said Apollo.

He walked to the next booth and waited in line. He came back with a plate of sticky rice with fried chicken and Hmong sausages.

"My favorite!" said Astrid. She picked a piece of sausage. She pressed it into a ball of sticky rice and gave it to Eliana.

Eliana made a face. "Yummy milk," she said.

"I don't know what you mean," said Astrid.

Apollo put the plate of rice and meat under the stroller seat.

"Let's go find Dad," he said.

As they walked toward the soccer fields, Eliana started to cry.

Astrid leaned down. "Sorry, Eliana. We don't know what to give you," she said.

Eliana cried harder.

Suddenly loud cheering came from the fields. People were standing up and clapping.

The players ran and hugged by the net. They were next to the tall pole.

Astrid and Apollo looked at the crowds.

"Apollo, it's field six! I think they won the game!" said Astrid.

"We missed it!" said Apollo.

CHAPTER 4

Bicycle Kick

"I can't believe we didn't get to see the game!" said Astrid, pushing the stroller.

Eliana was no longer sitting in it. She was on Apollo's back, still crying. He was giving her a piggyback ride.

Astrid followed them with the stroller.

"We should have been with Dad!" Apollo said.

"It's his favorite team!" said Astrid.

Eliana kept crying. "Yummy milk . . ." she said.

"What is yummy milk?" Apollo said.

"I wish I knew!" said Astrid.

They passed a little girl sitting on the grass. She was drinking coconut juice.

"What about a coconut?" Astrid said.

Apollo looked at the girl. "That's right! Coconuts have milk. The milk is yummy," he said.

"Over there!" said Astrid. Nearby was a booth selling whole coconuts. More desserts were on the counter.

"Let's try that," said Astrid.

"I'll get it!" said Apollo. He put Eliana on the ground and ran over to the booth.

When Apollo came back, he had fried bananas, mango on sticky rice, and a big coconut. A straw was sticking out of the top of the coconut.

"See the straw?" Apollo said to Eliana.

Eliana touched the coconut. She put the straw in her mouth.

Astrid crossed her fingers.

"Please, let this be it!" said Apollo.

Eliana pushed the straw away. She cried again.

Apollo hit his hand to his forehead. "I give up!" he said.

Astrid shrugged. Then she pointed to the soccer fields.

People were still cheering. A family walked by talking happily.

"Did that team just win?" Apollo asked them.

"Yes, it was a good game," the mom said. "They scored a goal at the last minute!"

"One guy did a header. The ball flew so high! Then another guy did a bicycle kick!" the son said.

"The goalie tried to block it but missed. They're going to the finals!" said the dad.

They laughed and talked loudly as they walked away.

Astrid sighed. "We missed a bicycle kick."

"And a header," said Apollo.

Suddenly Eliana pointed and screamed, "Yummy milk!"

Astrid and Apollo looked where she was pointing. They saw Dad sitting on a chair under a blue and white umbrella. He was on a field on the other side. He was holding a plastic cup and drinking from a big straw.

CHAPTER 5

Soccer Celebration

"Dad!" Astrid and Apollo said.

Dad turned and saw them. He waved.

Eliana ran toward him.

"Eliana, wait!" said Astrid.

"Slow down!" said Apollo.

They chased after her, but she was fast. Apollo ran behind her. Astrid followed quickly with the stroller.

When Eliana got to Dad, he lifted her in the air. Eliana cried and kicked her legs. Dad set her down.

"What's wrong?" he said.

Eliana grabbed Dad's plastic cup on the grass. She sucked on the straw.

Astrid and Apollo ran up to them. They watched Eliana with wide eyes.

Eliana swallowed. Then she smiled and said, "Yummy milk."

"That's yummy milk?" said Astrid.

"It's the tricolor dessert!" said Apollo.

Eliana showed them the plastic cup. It was filled with pink, green, and yellow tapioca pearls.

"Now I get it! The coconut cream is the milk. The pearls are the yummy!" said Astrid.

Eliana went back to Dad. He picked her up and said, "What happened?"

"She kept asking for yummy milk. We didn't know what it was," said Apollo.

Dad wiped Eliana's tears. "I came up with that name. The last time I bought some at the store, I gave it to her. She loved it."

Eliana hugged Dad.

"We should have guessed it," said Apollo.

"And Dad?" said Astrid. "We're sorry we missed your game."

Apollo nodded. "We wanted to watch your favorite team win. We wanted to celebrate with you."

"They didn't play yet," Dad said.

Astrid and Apollo looked at each other in surprise.

"But we heard people cheering for the team at field six," said Astrid.

"A family told us that team is going to the finals," Apollo said.

"Oh, that was another team. That was the Twirling Tornadoes," Dad said. "My favorite team is playing here, on field nine."

"Mom said you were on field six!" said Astrid.

"I wrote nine," Dad said, laughing. "Maybe the note was upside down. But you didn't miss the game. They're about to play now. See?"

Astrid and Apollo saw a new team come onto the field. They jogged onto the grass in two rows. They ran in place. Some of them did flips. People clapped.

Dad said, *"That's* my favorite team."

Astrid and Apollo watched them. Some players were stretching on the grass. Some were bouncing soccer balls on their knees and feet.

One player tossed a ball in the air and bounced it off his head. Everyone clapped again.

"We thought we wouldn't get to watch the game with you!" said Astrid.

Dad smiled. "You're just in time. I know they'll make it to the finals. They win every year."

Astrid and Apollo nodded.

"I am getting hungry, though," said Dad. "I could use some food."

"We can help with that!" said Apollo. He showed Dad Eliana's stroller.

Dad stared at all the food in the cup holders, the tray, and under the seat. "This is what I call a soccer celebration!"

Astrid and Apollo passed the food to Dad. Eliana sat on Dad's lap and drank the tricolor dessert.

Astrid bit into a beef stick. She said, "Dad, what's your favorite team?"

"We keep forgetting their name," said Apollo as he chewed on the fried chicken.

Dad ate a bite of papaya salad. "Wow, that's spicy!" He took a sip from the coconut. "My team is the Raging Riptide," he said.

Astrid and Apollo laughed.

"We were way off!" said Astrid.

Apollo shook his head. "We weren't even close!"

For the rest of the day, under a blue umbrella, Astrid, Apollo, and Eliana sat with Dad.

They ate barbecued meat, sausages, sticky rice, noodles, papaya salad, and sweet desserts. Eliana drank yummy milk. When the Raging Riptide won the game, they celebrated together.

- Hmong people first lived in southern China. Many of them moved to Southeast Asia in the 1800s. Some Hmong decided to stay in the country of Laos (pronounced *LAH-ohs*).

LAOS

- In the 1950s, a war called the Vietnam War started in Southeast Asia. The United States joined this war. They asked the Hmong in Laos to help them. When the U.S. lost the war, Hmong people had to leave Laos.

- After 1975, many Hmong came to the U.S. as refugees. Refugees are people who escape from their country to find a new, safe place to live. Today, Minnesota is home to around 85,000 Hmong.

- Every summer, a large soccer festival is held in St. Paul, Minnesota, during the July Fourth holiday. Besides soccer, other sports are played at the event. This is the biggest sports festival for Hmong Americans. Almost 60,000 people attend! Best of all, people sell delicious food at the festival.

POPULAR FOOD
AT THE HMONG SOCCER FESTIVAL

barbecued meat sticks—grilled beef, pork, chicken, or other meat on a stick

fried bananas—bananas fried in a crunchy dough

khao poon—a popular noodle dish with a red curry soup. This dish is from Laos and Thailand. Chicken, cabbage, pepper, and other spices are usually mixed into the soup.

mango on sticky rice—slices of mango on sticky rice flavored with coconut milk

pho—a noodle dish from Vietnam. Beef, onions, basil, and other herbs can be added to the noodles in beef broth.

tapioca pearls—little chewy balls made from the starch of a vegetable called cassava

tricolor dessert—a dessert from Southeast Asia made of tapioca pearls in coconut milk and sugar syrup. It is also called *nam van*. Fruits, jelly, and other sweet ingredients are mixed in the dessert. Many Hmong children (and adults) love this dessert!

whole coconut—a young coconut that still has juice inside. If the top is cut off, you can drink the juice.

basil (BAY-zuhl)—an herb used in cooking

bicycle kick (BYE-si-kuhl KIK)—a kick in soccer where the player jumps backward into the air, kicking the ball when it is above them in midair

celebration (sel-uh-BRAY-shuhn)—a party or gathering, usually to mark a big event

cucumber (KYOO-kuhm-bur)—a long green vegetable with a soft center

festival (FES-tuh-vuhl)—a party or holiday

goalie (GOH-lee)—someone who guards the goal in soccer to prevent the other team from scoring

header (HED-er)—in soccer, the act of hitting the ball with your head

picnic (PIK-nik)—a party that includes a meal eaten outside

piggyback (PIG-ee-bak)—carried on the back or shoulders

rescue (RES-kyoo)—to save someone who is in danger

snowflake (SNOH-flake)—a single flake of snow

syrup (SIR-uhp)—a thick, sweet liquid made by boiling sugar and water

V.T. Bidania was born in Laos and grew up in St. Paul, Minnesota. She spent most of her childhood writing stories, and now that she's an adult, she is thrilled to be writing stories for children. She has an MFA in Creative Writing from The New School and is a recipient of the Loft Literary Center's Mirrors and Windows Fellowship. She lives outside of the Twin Cities with her family.

Dara Lashia Lee is a Hmong American illustrator based in the Twin Cities in Minnesota. She utilizes digital media to create semi-realistic illustrations ranging from Japanese anime to western cartoon styles. Her Hmong-inspired illustrations were displayed at the Qhia Dab Neeg (Storytelling) touring exhibit from 2015 to 2018. When she's not drawing, she likes to travel, take silly photos of her cat, and drink bubble tea.

1. Why were Astrid and Apollo so excited about the soccer festival? What were all the things they wanted to do when they got there?

2. The papaya salad dish was very spicy. What did Astrid and Apollo do to make the spicy taste go away? Talk about a time when you ate something that had a very strong taste.

3. Astrid and Apollo could not understand Eliana when she said, "Yummy milk!" Discuss all the things they did to try to make her happy.

1. The twins' dad wrote a note to tell them where to meet him. Write a note to a friend telling them where to meet you at a crowded event. Make a map and give directions so they can find you easily.

2. Astrid and Apollo talked about bicycle kicks in soccer. Write a list of soccer moves or moves from another sport you like. Draw a picture of yourself doing a bicycle kick or your favorite sports move.

3. Pretend you are Astrid or Apollo. Write a poem about the soccer festival. Write about the people you see, the weather, colors, sounds, and smells. Write about something yummy you ate and how it tasted!